A GIFT FOR

_____

FROM

_____

Published in Nashville, Tennessee, by Tommy Nelson. Tommy Nelson is an imprint of Thomas Nelson. Thomas Nelson is a registered trademark of HarperCollins Christian Publishing, Inc.

Illustrated by Natalia Moore

Interior design by Christina Quintero

Tommy Nelson titles may be purchased in bulk for educational, business, fund-raising, or sales promotional use. For information, please e-mail SpecialMarkets@ThomasNelson.com.

Unless otherwise noted, Scripture quotations are taken from the Holy Bible, New International Version®, NIV®. Copyright © 1973, 1978, 1984, 2011 by Biblica, Inc.™ Used by permission of Zondervan. All rights reserved worldwide. www.zondervan.com

ISBN-13: 978-1-4003-2419-4

Library of Congress Cataloging-in-Publication Data is on file.

Printed in China

14 15 16 17 18 DSC 6 5 4 3 2 1

Mfr: DSC / Shenzhen, China / September 2014 / PO #9307236

It will be Okay

Trusting GOD through fear and change

Lysa TerKeurst

illustrated by Natalia Moore

A Division of Thomas Nelson Publishers

Hi Friend,

One of the hardest life lessons for me to teach my kids has been on fear and worry. As their mom, I feel what they feel. I hurt when they hurt. I worry about their worries!

When one of my daughters was seven, she suddenly became afraid to get up on a stage in front of her school. This was something she'd loved before, yet anxiety was paralyzing her now. As we drove to school, I told her I'd sit on the front row so she could keep her eyes locked on me. My presence could give her reassurance and my smile could give her courage.

It worked great because I was there in person. But as my kids have grown, I've had to get more creative. I've been intentional in helping them find this same assurance and courage to face their fears by keeping their eyes on God and turning to Scripture.

And that is where I needed a story to illustrate how we can trust God in the midst of fear and understand He is still good even when life doesn't feel good.

Oh, how my mommy heart is praying for you and your kids as you read this book. I'm praying for you as you translate this story into the unique fears and worries your kids are facing today. And then hopefully they can carry this lesson into the days ahead that will no longer end with bedtime stories.

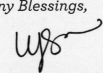

I've also written out a list of Scripture memory verses that will be helpful to tuck into your kids' hearts or stick on their mirror and equip them with the most powerful tool—God's Word!

Many Blessings,

10 Scriptures to Memorize with Your Kids

Do not be anxious about anything, but in every situation, by prayer and petition, with thanksgiving, present your requests to God.
PHILIPPIANS 4:6

And we know that in all things God works for the good of those who love him, who have been called according to his purpose.
ROMANS 8:28

"I am with you and will watch over you wherever you go."
GENESIS 28:15

The LORD your God is with you, the Mighty Warrior who saves.
ZEPHANIAH 3:17

"For I know the plans I have for you," declares the LORD, "plans to prosper you and not to harm you, plans to give you hope and a future."
JEREMIAH 29:11

"So do not fear, for I am with you; do not be dismayed, for I am your God. I will strengthen you and help you; I will uphold you with my righteous right hand."
ISAIAH 41:10

When I am afraid, I put my trust in you. In God, whose word I praise—in God I trust and am not afraid.
PSALM 56:3–4

Be strong and courageous. Do not be afraid or terrified because of them, for the LORD your God goes with you; he will never leave you nor forsake you.
DEUTERONOMY 31:6

We take captive every thought to make it obedient to Christ.
2 CORINTHIANS 10:5

I love you, LORD, my strength. The LORD is my rock, my fortress and my deliverer; my God is my rock, in whom I take refuge, my shield and the horn of my salvation, my stronghold.
PSALM 18:1–2

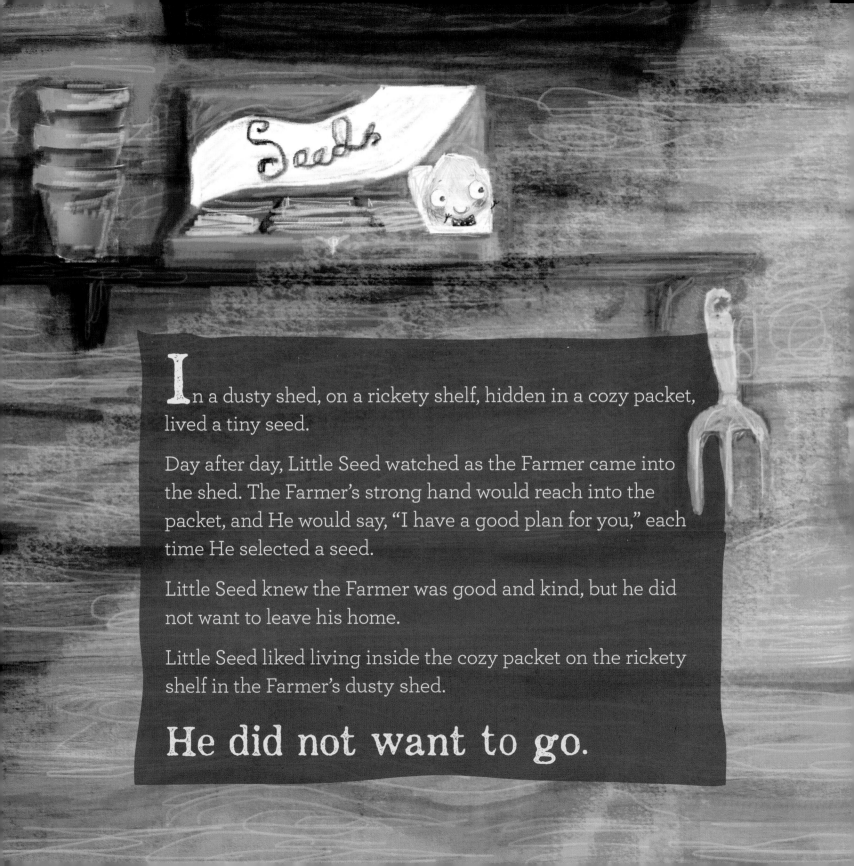

In a dusty shed, on a rickety shelf, hidden in a cozy packet, lived a tiny seed.

Day after day, Little Seed watched as the Farmer came into the shed. The Farmer's strong hand would reach into the packet, and He would say, "I have a good plan for you," each time He selected a seed.

Little Seed knew the Farmer was good and kind, but he did not want to leave his home.

Little Seed liked living inside the cozy packet on the rickety shelf in the Farmer's dusty shed.

He did not want to go.

In the nearby woods under the big, tall trees, in a comfy den, lived a playful fox.

Little Fox raced around the tree trunks in the woods.

"Yippee!"

he shouted with glee.

But then a long, black shadow scared him, and he hurried to
hide in his den. He was scared of the dark shadows.

And howling winds.
And rain.
And most everything.

Little Fox liked his comfy den under the big, tall trees
in the nearby woods.

He did not like
being afraid.

One particularly dark night, a storm rumbled into the forest. Thunder boomed. Lightning flashed. Rain poured into Little Fox's den.

"Oh no!"

Little Fox cried as he scurried through the woods, trying to find somewhere safe and dry and not scary. He barreled inside the Farmer's dusty shed, bumped into the rickety shelf, and knocked over the cozy seed packet.

Little Seed rolled out onto the floor.

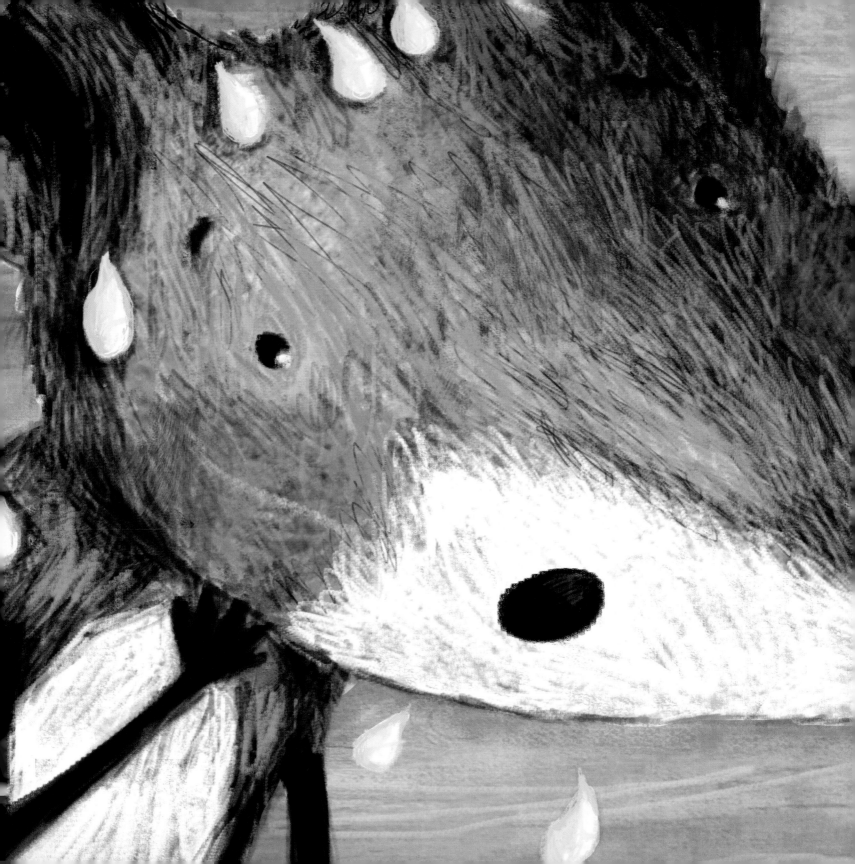

A surprised Little Fox found himself standing nose to nose with a very unhappy Little Seed.

"I am Little Fox, and I live in the den under the big, tall trees in the nearby woods," he explained. "I love to play in the woods . . . but I'm afraid of dark shadows and howling winds," he said. "There are no winds or shadows in your shed. Can I live here with you?

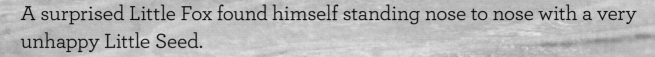

Little Seed said, "Do you see a pillow? Do you see a bed? Do you see a place to lay your wet head? No, you don't! Because this safe place is the Farmer's shed."

But then Little Seed thought of how safe and warm it was inside the cozy packet on the rickety shelf in the Farmer's dusty shed. He thought it might be quite nice to have a friend.

Little Fox and Little Seed became the best of friends.

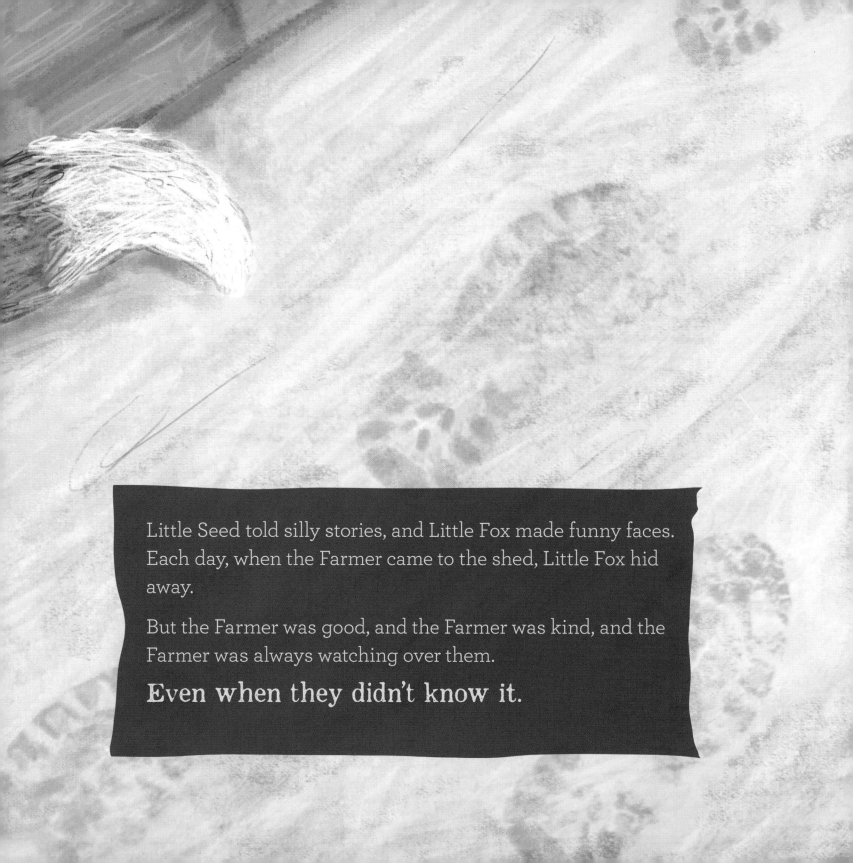

Little Seed told silly stories, and Little Fox made funny faces. Each day, when the Farmer came to the shed, Little Fox hid away.

But the Farmer was good, and the Farmer was kind, and the Farmer was always watching over them.

Even when they didn't know it.

One morning, the Farmer came into the shed, as He had on many days.

"Little Seed," He said as He placed him in His hand, "I have a wonderful plan for you. I have waited for just the right time, and today is the day!"

Oh no, please no! I don't want to go!

thought Little Seed.

The Farmer went outside and knelt down. He pushed Little Seed under the ground, into the dirt, and down to a deep, dark, messy place.

"Now, Little Seed, this is going to be different and it might seem scary, but it will be okay. You can trust Me," said the Farmer.

Little Seed wished he were inside the cozy packet on the rickety shelf in the Farmer's dusty shed.

"I want to trust, even when I can't see.
But how in the world is this good for me?"

"Little Seed, come back!"

cried Little Fox when he saw the Farmer take his friend away. "Where are you, Little Seed?"

He looked in the front of the shed and behind the shed, but . . .

Little Seed was not there.

He looked on top of the tractor and under the tractor, but . . .

Little Seed was not there either.

He looked under the duck's wings

and inside the dog's floppy ears.

He looked in the horse's stall, the pig's pen,
and even in the Farmer's boot, but . . .

Little Seed could not be found anywhere!

Now Little Fox was really worried. **"Little Seed?"** he shouted.

"I'm here, I'm here,

way down in the dirt.

I'm scared and I'm lonely, but I'm not hurt,"

came Little Seed's muffled voice right below him.

Little Fox thought hard for something to say or something to do that would help his friend not be scared. But he was afraid too.

"It's different and scary to be someplace new ... but it will be okay, Little Seed."

Little Seed was not so sure. And neither was Little Fox.

But the Farmer was good, and the Farmer was kind, and the Farmer was always watching over them.

Even when they didn't know it.

Little Fox stayed by Little Seed night after night and day after day. **He was scared and lonely too.**

But after a while Little Fox started to see how the Farmer took care of them. Fresh water for Little Seed. Sweet berries for Little Fox. He wasn't even quite so afraid when he saw the dark shadows or heard the howling wind. Little Fox was starting to believe that the Farmer was good, and the Farmer was kind.

"My friend," whispered a sleepy Little Fox to Little Seed, "go to sleep.

"It will be okay."

Little Seed sat in that dark and messy place
for what seemed like a very long time.

But one spring morning, Little Seed felt a
mysterious stirring. He looked down and
discovered he was no longer a little seed;
he was becoming something brand-new—
something wonderful!

He pushed up through the dark, out
of the dirt, and right through the ground!

And there, looking sleepy-eyed and surprised, was his friend,

Little Fox.

Little Fox looked down and saw a beautiful green sprout.

"My friend!"

they each exclaimed with glee. They were once again nose to nose, and Little Seed told silly stories, and Little Fox made funny faces.

After many days of fun, Little Seed said,

"Little Fox, look up and see!
It's hard to believe what's become of me.
From the messy, dark place I grew and grew.
From a seed to a tree—only the Farmer knew."

Together they made it through the dark and
scary time, and together they each learned
that the Farmer was good, and
the Farmer was kind, and the
Farmer was always watching
over them.

Even in dark, messy places.

Little Seed was never supposed to just be a seed in a seed packet. And Little Fox was not supposed to be alone and afraid. The seasons came, and the seasons went.

Little Seed grew into a big, strong tree.

And Little Fox raced around his tree trunk. And sometimes, Little Fox lay in the tall, cool grass near Little Seed.

And the breeze tickled his nose, and the sun warmed his belly.

And the good and kind Farmer was always watching over them.

Little Seed liked things
to stay the way they were.

Little Fox was sometimes
afraid.

But just as they learned to trust the Farmer, we can
learn to trust God.

We do not need to fear. He has a wonderful plan.

God loves you, and He is kind.

And in the end, it really will be okay.

Trust this truth in the tough things you face.

Confusing times in the messy, hard place.

God loves you, and He is kind.

Remember this always in your heart and your mind.